The Secret Garden

(ABRIDGED)

FRANCES HODGSON BURNETT

Illustrated by Thea Kliros

DOVER PUBLICATIONS, INC.
New York

DOVER CHILDREN'S THRIFT CLASSICS

EDITOR OF THIS VOLUME: THOMAS CROFTS

Bibliographical Note

This Dover edition, first published in 1994, is a new abridgment of *The Secret Garden* (first publication: William Heinemann, London, 1911). The illustrations and introductory Note have been specially prepared for the present edition. The abridgment was specially prepared by Bob Blaisdell.

Library of Congress Cataloging-in-Publication Data

Burnett, Frances Hodgson, 1849–1924.
    The secret garden / Frances Hodgson Burnett ; illustrated by Thea Kliros.
        p.   cm. — (Dover children's thrift classics)
    "Abridged."
    Summary: Ten-year-old Mary comes to live in a lonely house on the Yorkshire moors and discovers an invalid cousin and the mysteries of a locked garden.
    ISBN 0-486-28024-1 (pbk.)
    [1. Orphans—Fiction. 2. Gardens—Fiction. 3. Physically handicapped—Fiction. 4. Yorkshire (England)—Fiction.] I. Kliros, Thea, ill. II. Title. III. Series.
PZ7.B934Se   1994
[Fic]—dc20
                                   94-1185
                                      CIP
                                      AC

Manufactured in the United States of America
Dover Publications, Inc., 31 East 2nd Street, Mineola, N.Y. 11501

Note

In *The Secret Garden*, Frances Hodgson Burnett's most popular and enduring work, a disagreeable young orphan named Mary is brought to live with her uncle in a great mansion called Misselthwaite. Only, her uncle is never home, the people around her speak in a strange dialect and her new surroundings seem utterly unsympathetic to her. A general unhappiness seems to hang over the whole house. But as spring arrives, and a certain garden is discovered at Misselthwaite, things begin to change magically for Mary, and for her new companions.

This story, which was first published in 1911, was inspired by the author's own garden at her home in Kent, England. In turn, the story itself has had such an effect upon its readers that one of them, Celia, Lady Scarborough, created her own Secret Garden at her house in Yorkshire.

List of Illustrations

PAGE

"What is that?" she said, pointing out of
   the window. 7

She was standing *inside* the secret garden. . 30

On the bed was lying a boy, crying pitifully. . 43

There was every joy on earth in the secret
   garden that morning. 56

"I'm not a cripple!" Colin cried out. 72

A boy burst through the door at full speed. . 83

WHEN MARY Lennox was sent to Misselthwaite Manor to live with her uncle, everybody said she was the most disagreeable-looking child ever seen. She had a little thin face and a little thin body, thin light hair and a sour expression. Her hair was yellow, and her face was yellow because she had been born in India and had always been ill in one way or another. Her father had held a position under the English Government and her mother had been a great beauty. When Mary was born her mother handed her over to the care of an Ayah, a native servant. By the time Mary was six years old she was as tyrannical and selfish a little pig as ever lived.

One morning when she was about nine years old, she awakened feeling very cross. Nothing was done in its regular order and several of the regular servants, including her Ayah, seemed missing. The cholera had broken out in its most fatal form and people were dying like flies.

During the confusion and bewilderment of the second day Mary hid herself in the nursery and was forgotten by everyone. Mary alternately cried and slept through the hours.

When she awakened after a long sleep she lay and stared at the wall. She heard neither voices nor footsteps, and wondered if everybody had got well of the cholera and all the trouble was over. Mary was standing in the middle of the nursery when two men opened the door a few minutes later. She looked an ugly, cross little thing and was frowning because she was beginning to be hungry and feel disgracefully neglected.

"I am Mary Lennox," Mary said. "I fell asleep when everyone had the cholera and I have only just wakened up. Why does nobody come?"

"Poor little kid!" one of the men said. "There is nobody left to come."

It was in that strange and sudden way that Mary found out that she had neither father nor mother left.

If Mary had been older she would no doubt have been very anxious at being left alone in the world, but she was very young, and as she had always been taken care of, she supposed she always would be.

She knew that she was not going to stay at the English clergyman's house in India where she was taken at first. The clergyman was

poor and he had five children all nearly the
same age and they wore shabby clothes. Mary
hated their untidy bungalow and was so disagreeable to them that after the first day or
two nobody would play with her. By the second day they had given her a nickname which
made her furious.

It was Basil who thought of it first. Basil
was a little boy with blue eyes and a turned-
up nose, and Mary hated him. She was playing
by herself under a tree, making heaps of earth
and paths for a garden and Basil came and
stood near to watch her.

"Go away!" cried Mary. "I don't want boys.
Go away!"

He danced round and round her and made
faces and sang and laughed.

> *Mistress Mary, quite contrary,*
> *How does your garden grow?*
> *With silver bells, and cockle shells,*
> *And marigolds all in a row.*

He sang it until the other children heard
and laughed, too; and the crosser Mary got,
the more they sang "Mistress Mary Quite Contrary"; and after that as long as she stayed
with them they called her "Mistress Mary
Quite Contrary."

"You are going to be sent home," Basil said

to her, "at the end of the week. And we're glad of it."

"I am glad of it, too," answered Mary. "Where is home?"

"It's England, of course. You are going to your uncle. His name is Mr. Archibald Craven. He lives in a great, big, old house in the country. He's a hunchback, and he's horrid."

Mary made the long voyage to England under the care of an officer's wife who handed the child over to the woman Mr. Archibald Craven sent to meet her in London. The woman was his housekeeper at Misselthwaite Manor, Mrs. Medlock. She was a stout woman, with very red cheeks and sharp black eyes.

When the next day Mary and Mrs. Medlock set out on their journey to Yorkshire, Mary sat in her corner of the railway carriage. She had nothing to read or to look at, and she had folded her thin little black-gloved hands in her lap.

"I suppose I may as well tell you something about where you are going to," Mrs. Medlock said. "You are going to a queer place. Not but that it's a grand big place in a gloomy way. The house is six hundred years old, and it's on the edge of the moor, and there's near a hundred rooms in it, though most of them's shut up and locked. And there's pictures and fine old furniture and things that's been there for ages, and there's a big park round it and gardens and trees. But there's nothing else. *He's* not going to trouble himself about you, that's sure and certain. He never troubles himself about no one. He's got a crooked back. That set him wrong. He was a sour young man and got no good of all his money and big place till he was married. She was a sweet, pretty young thing, and he'd have walked the world over to get her a blade o' grass she wanted. When she died—"

"Oh! did she die?" Mary exclaimed.

"Yes, she died," Mrs. Medlock answered. "And it made him queerer than ever. He cares about nobody. Most of the time he goes away, and when he is at Misselthwaite he shuts himself up in the West Wing. You'll have to play about and look after yourself. You'll be told what rooms you can go into and what rooms you're to keep out of. There's gardens enough. But when you're in the house don't go wandering and poking about."

When they arrived at Misselthwaite Manor that night a neat, thin old man stood near the manservant who opened the door for them. "You are to take her to her room," he said to Mrs. Medlock. "He doesn't want to see her.

He's going to London in the morning."

And then Mary Lennox was led up a broad staircase and down a long corridor and up a short flight of steps and through another corridor and another, until a door opened in a wall and she found herself in a room with a fire in it and a supper on the table.

"Well, here you are," said Mrs. Medlock. "This room and the next are where you'll live—and you must keep to them. Don't you forget that!"

It was in this way that Mistress Mary arrived at Misselthwaite Manor, and she had perhaps never felt quite so contrary in all her life.

When Mary opened her eyes in the morning it was because a young housemaid had come into her room to light the fire and was kneeling on the hearth-rug raking out the cinders noisily. Mary lay and watched her for a few moments and then began to look about the room. Out of a deep window she could see a great climbing stretch of land which seemed to have no trees on it, and to look rather like an endless, dull, purplish sea.

"What is that?" she said, pointing out of the window.

Martha, the young housemaid, who had just

"What is that?" she said, pointing out of the
window.

risen to her feet, looked, and pointed also.

"That there?" she said.

"Yes."

"That's th' moor. Does tha' like it?"

"No," answered Mary. "I hate it."

"That's because tha'rt not used to it," Martha said going back to her hearth. "Tha' thinks it's too big an' bare now. But tha' will like it."

"Do you?" inquired Mary.

"Aye, that I do," answered Martha. "I just love it. It's none bare. It's covered wi' growin' things as smells sweet. It's fair lovely in spring an' summer. It smells o' honey an' there's such a lot o' fresh air—an' th' sky looks so high an' th' bees an' skylarks makes such a nice noise hummin' an' singin'."

Mary listened to her with a grave, puzzled expression. The native servants she had been used to in India were not in the least like this.

"Are you going to be my servant?" Mary asked.

"I'm Mrs. Medlock's servant," Martha said. "And she's Mr. Craven's—but I'm to do the housemaid's work up here an' wait on you a bit. But you won't need much waitin' on."

"Who is going to dress me?" demanded Mary.

Martha stared. She spoke in broad Yorkshire in her amazement. "Canna' tha' dress thysen?"

"What do you mean? I don't understand your language," said Mary.

"Eh!" Martha said. "I mean can't you put on your own clothes?"

"No," answered Mary. "I never did in my life. My Ayah dressed me, of course."

"Well," said Martha, "it's time tha' should learn. My mother always said she couldn't see why grand people's children didn't turn out fair fools—what with nurses an' bein' washed an' dressed an' took out to walk as if they was puppies!"

"It's different in India," said Mistress Mary. She felt so hopeless before the girl's simple stare, and somehow she felt so horribly lonely and far away from everything she understood and which understood her; that she threw herself face downward on the pillows and burst into passionate sobbing.

"Eh! you mustn't cry like that there!" Martha begged. "You mustn't for sure. Do stop cryin'."

There was something comforting and really friendly in Martha's Yorkshire speech and sturdy way which had a good effect on Mary. She gradually ceased crying and became quiet. Martha looked relieved.

"It's time for thee to get up now," she said. "Mrs. Medlock said I was to carry tha' breakfast an' tea an' dinner into th' room next to this. I'll help thee on with thy clothes if tha'll get out of bed."

The dressing process was one which taught them both something.

"Why doesn't tha' put on tha' own shoes?" Martha said when Mary quietly held out her foot.

"My Ayah did it," answered Mary. "It was the custom."

It had not been the custom that Mistress Mary should do anything but stand and allow herself to be dressed like a doll, but before she was ready for breakfast she began to suspect that her life at Misselthwaite Manor would end by teaching her a number of things quite new to her—things such as putting on her own shoes and stockings, and picking up things she let fall.

At first Mary was not at all interested in Martha's readiness to talk about her family, but gradually, as the girl rattled on in her good-tempered way, Mary began to notice what she was saying.

"Eh! you should see 'em all," said Martha. "There's twelve of us an' my father only gets sixteen shilling' a week. I can tell you my mother's put to it to get porridge for 'em all. They tumble about on th' moor an' play there all day, an' mother says th' air of th' moor fattens 'em. She says she believes they eat th' grass same as th' wild ponies do. Our Dickon, he's twelve years old and he's got a young pony he calls his own."

"Where did he get it?" asked Mary.

"He found it on th' moor with its mother when it was a little one, an' he began to make friends with it an' give it bits o' bread an' pluck young grass for it. And it got to like him so it follows him about an' lets him get on its back. Dickon's a kind lad an' animals like him."

Mary had never possessed an animal pet of her own and had always thought she should like one. So she began to feel a slight interest in Dickon. When she went into the room which had been made into a nursery for her, she found that it was like the one she had slept in. It was not a child's room, but a grown-up person's room, with gloomy old pictures on the walls and heavy old oak chairs. A table in the center was set with a good, substantial breakfast, but she looked with something more than indifference at the first plate Martha set before her.

"I don't want it," she said.

"Tha' doesn't want thy porridge!" Martha exclaimed.

"No."

"Tha' doesn't know how good it is. Put a bit o' treacle on it or a bit o' sugar."

"I don't want it," repeated Mary.

Mary drank some tea and ate a little toast and some marmalade.

"You wrap up warm an' run out an' play you," said Martha. "It'll do you good and give you some stomach for your meat."

Mary went to the window. There were gardens and paths and big trees, but everything looked dull and wintry.

"Out? Why should I go out on a day like this?"

"Well, if tha' doesn't go out tha'lt have to stay in, an' what has tha' got to do?"

"Who will go with me?"

"You'll go by yourself," Martha answered. "You'll have to learn to play like other children does when they haven't got sisters and brothers. Our Dickon goes off on th' moor by himself an' plays for hours."

Martha found her coat and hat for her and a pair of stout little boots and she showed her the way downstairs.

"If tha' goes round that way tha'll come to th' gardens," she said, pointing to a gate in a wall of shrubbery. "There's lots o' flowers in summer-time, but there's nothin' bloomin' now." She seemed to hesitate a second before she added, "One of th' gardens is locked up. No one has been in it for ten years."

"Why?" asked Mary.

"Mr. Craven had it shut when his wife died so sudden. He won't let no one go inside. It was her garden. He locked th' door an' dug a hole and buried th' key."

After she was gone Mary turned down the walk which led to the door in the shrubbery. She could not help thinking about the garden which no one had been into for ten years. She wondered what it would look like and whether there were any flowers still alive in it. When she had passed through the shrubbery gate she found herself in great gardens, with wide lawns and winding walks with clipped borders. There were trees, and flower-beds, and evergreens clipped into strange shapes, and a large pool with an old gray fountain in its midst. But the flower-beds were bare and wintry and the fountain was not playing. This was not the garden which was shut up.

She saw, at the end of the path she was following, there seemed to be a long wall, with ivy growing over it. She went towards the wall and found that there was a green door in the ivy, and that it stood open. This was not the closed garden evidently, and she could go into it.

She went through the door and found that it was a garden with walls all around it and that it was only one of several walled gardens which seemed to open into one another. She saw another open green door, revealing bushes and pathways between beds containing winter vegetables. Fruit-trees were trained flat against the wall, and over some of the beds there were glass frames.

Presently an old man with a spade over his shoulder walked through the door leading from the second garden. He had a surly old face, and did not seem at all pleased to see Mary.

"What is this place?" she asked.

"One o' th' kitchen gardens," he answered.

"What is that?" said Mary, pointing through the other green door.

"Another of 'em. There's another on t'other side o' th' wall an' there's th' orchard t'other side o' that."

"Can I go in them?" asked Mary.

"If tha' likes. But there's nowt to see."

Mary made no response. She went down and through the second green door. There she found more walls and winter vegetables and glass frames, but in the second wall there was another green door and it was not open. Perhaps it led into the garden which no one had seen for ten years. She hoped the door would not open, because she wanted to be sure she had found the mysterious garden—but it did open quite easily and she walked through it and found herself in an orchard. There were walls all around it also and trees trained against them, and there were bare fruit-trees growing in the winter-browned grass—but there was no green door to be seen anywhere. Mary looked for it, and yet when she had entered the upper end of the garden she had noticed that the wall did not seem to end with the orchard, but to extend beyond it as if it enclosed a place at the other side. She could see the tops of trees above the wall, and when she stood still she saw a bird with a bright red breast sitting on the topmost branch of one of them, and suddenly he burst into his winter song.

She stopped and listened to him until he flew away.

She walked back into the first kitchen-garden she had entered and found the old man digging there. She went and stood beside him and watched him a few moments in her cold little way. He took no notice of her, and so at last she spoke to him.

"I have been into the other gardens," she said. "I went into the orchard. There was no door there into the other garden."

"What garden?"

"The one on the other side of the wall," answered Mistress Mary. "There were trees there—I saw the tops of them. A bird with a red breast was sitting on one of them, and he sang."

The gardener smiled and turned about to the orchard side of his garden and began to whistle—a low, soft whistle.

Almost the next moment she heard a soft little rushing flight through the air—and it was the bird with the red breast flying to them, and he actually alighted on the big clod of earth quite near to the gardener's foot.

"Here he is," chuckled the old man.

The bird put his tiny head on one side and looked up at him with his soft bright eye, which was like a black dewdrop. He seemed quite familiar and not the least afraid. He hopped about and pecked the earth briskly, looking for seeds and insects. He had a tiny plump body and a delicate beak, and slender delicate legs.

"What kind of bird is he?" Mary asked.

"Doesn't tha' know? He's a robin redbreast,

an' they're th' friendliest, curiousest birds alive. The old ones turn 'em out o' their nest an' make 'em fly, an' they're scattered before you know it. This one was a knowin' one an' he knew he was lonely."

Mistress Mary went a step nearer to the robin and looked at him very hard. "I'm lonely," she said.

She had not known before that this was one of the things which made her feel sour and cross. She seemed to find it out when the robin looked at her and she looked at the robin.

The gardener began to dig again.

"What is your name?" Mary inquired.

"Ben Weatherstaff," he answered. "I'm lonely mysel' except when he's with me," and he jerked his thumb towards the robin. "He's th' only friend I've got."

"I have no friends at all," said Mary. "I never had. My Ayah didn't like me and I never played with anyone."

"Tha' an' me are a good bit alike," said Ben. "We was wove out of th' same cloth. We're neither of us good-lookin' an' we're both of us as sour as we look. We've got the same nasty tempers, both of us, I'll warrant."

Suddenly a clear rippling little sound broke out near her and she turned round. She was standing a few feet from a young apple-tree, and the robin had flown on to one of its branches and had burst out into a scrap of a song.

"What did he do that for?" asked Mary.

"He's made up his mind to make friends with thee," replied Ben. "Dang me if he hasn't took a fancy to thee."

"To me?" said Mary, and she moved towards the little tree and looked up.

"Would you make friends with me?" she said to the robin. "Would you?"

"Why," Ben cried out, "tha' said that as nice an' human as if tha' was a real child instead of a sharp old woman. Tha' said it almost like Dickon talks to his wild things on th' moor."

Mary was almost as curious about Dickon as she was about the deserted garden. But just at that moment the robin, who had ended his song, gave a little shake of his wings, spread them, and flew away. He had made his visit and had other things to do.

"He has flown over the wall!" Mary cried out. "He has flown into the orchard—he has flown across the other wall—into the garden where there is no door!"

"He lives there," said old Ben. "He came out o' th' egg there. If he's courtin', he's makin' up to some young madam of a robin that lives among th' old rose-trees there."

"Rose-trees," said Mary. "Are there rose-trees?"

"That was ten year' ago," said Ben.

"I should like to see them," said Mary. "Where is the green door? There must be a door somewhere."

"There was ten year' ago, but there isn't now," he said.

"No door!" cried Mary. "There must be."

"None as anyone can find, an' none as is anyone's business. Don't be a meddlesome wench an' poke your nose where it's no cause to go. Here, I must go on with my work. Get you gone an' play you. I've no more time."

And he threw his spade over his shoulder and walked off, without even glancing at her or saying good-bye.

After a few days spent almost entirely out of doors, Mary wakened one morning knowing what it was to be hungry, and when she sat down to her breakfast she did not push the porridge away, but took up her spoon until her bowl was empty.

"It's th' air of th' moor givin' thee stomach for tha' victuals," said Martha. "You go on playin' you out o' doors every day an' you'll get some flesh on your bones an' you won't be so yeller."

That day Mary walked round and round the

gardens and wandered about the paths in the park. One place she went to oftener than to any other. It was the long walk outside the gardens with the walls round them. There were bare flower-beds on either side of it and against the walls the ivy grew thickly.

She stayed out of doors nearly all day, and when she sat down to her supper at night she felt hungry and drowsy and comfortable. She asked Martha, "Why did Mr. Craven hate the garden?"

"Listen to th' wind wutherin' round the house. You could bare stand up on the moor if you was out on it tonight."

Mary did not know what "wutherin'" meant until she listened, and then she understood. It must mean that hollow, shuddering sort of roar which rushed round and round the house.

"But why did he hate it so?" Mary persisted.

"Mind," said Martha, "Mrs. Medlock said it's not to be talked about. His troubles are none servants' business, he says. But for th' garden he wouldn't be like he is. It was Mrs. Craven's garden that she had made when first they were married an' she just loved it, an' they used to tend the flowers themselves. An' none o' th' gardeners was ever let to go in. Him an' her used to go in an' shut th' door an' stay there hours an' hours readin' an' talkin'. An' she was just a bit of a girl an' there was an old tree with a branch bent like a seat on it. An' she made roses grow over it an' she used to sit there. But one day when she was sittin' there th' branch broke an' she fell on th' ground an' was hurt so bad that next day she died. Th' doctors thought he'd go out o' his mind an' die, too. That's why he hates it. No one's never gone in since, an' he won't let anyone talk about it."

Mary looked at the fire and listened to the wind "wutherin'." But as she was listening she began to listen to something else. At first she could scarcely distinguish it from the wind itself. It seemed almost as if a child were crying somewhere. It was far away, but it was inside. She turned round and looked at Martha.

"Do you hear anyone crying?" she said.

"No," Martha answered. "It's the wind. Sometimes it sounds as if someone was lost on th' moor an' wailin'. It's got all sorts o' sounds."

"But listen," said Mary. "It's in the house— down one of those long corridors."

And at that very moment a door must have been opened somewhere downstairs; for a great rushing draft blew along the passage and the crying sound was swept down the far corridor, so that it was to be heard more plainly than ever.

"There!" said Mary. "I told you so! It is someone crying—and it isn't a grown-up person."

Martha ran and shut the door. "It was th' wind," said Martha. "An' if it wasn't, it was th' scullery-maid. She's had th' toothache all day."

But something troubled and awkward in her manner made Mistress Mary not believe Martha was speaking the truth.

Mary went and sat on the hearth-rug. "There *was* someone crying—there *was*— there *was!*" she said to herself. She had heard it, and some time she would find out.

Two mornings after this, when Mary opened her eyes she sat upright in bed immediately, and called to Martha.

"Look at the moor! Look at the moor!"

The rain-storm had ended and the gray mist and clouds had been swept away in the night by the wind. A brilliant, deep blue sky arched high over the moorland. The far-reaching world of the moor itself looked softly blue instead of gloomy purple-black or awful dreary gray.

"Aye," said Martha. "Yorkshire's th' sunniest

place on earth when it is sunny. I told thee tha'd like th' moor after a bit. Just you wait till you see th' gold-colored gorse blossoms an' th' blossom o' th' broom, an' th' heather flowerin', all purple bells, an' hundreds o' butterflies flutterin' an' bees hummin' an' skylarks soarin' up an' singin'. You'll want to get out on it at sunrise an' live on it all day like Dickon does."

"I like Dickon," said Mary. "And I've never seen him."

"Well," said Martha, "I wonder what Dickon would think of thee?"

"He wouldn't like me," said Mary. "No one does."

"How does tha' like thysel'?"

"Not at all—really," she answered. "But I never thought of that before."

"Mother said that to me once," said Martha. "I was in a bad temper an' talkin' ill of folk an' she turns round on me an' says: 'Tha' young vixen, tha'! How does tha' like thysel'?' It made me laugh an' it brought me to my senses in a minute."

Martha went away in high spirits as soon as she had given Mary her breakfast. She was going to walk five miles across the moor to her family's cottage, and she was going to help her mother with the washing and do the week's baking and enjoy herself thoroughly.

Mary felt lonelier than ever. She went out into the garden. The sunshine made the whole place look different. She went into the first kitchen-garden and found Ben Weatherstaff working there.

"Springtime's coming," he said. "Cannot tha' smell it?"

"I smell something nice and fresh and damp," she said.

"That's th' good rich earth," he answered, digging away. "It's in a good humor makin' ready to grow things. It's glad when plantin' time comes. In the flower gardens out there things will be stirrin' down below in th' dark. Th' sun's warmin' em. You'll see bits o' green spikes stickin' out o' th' black earth after a bit."

"What will they be?" asked Mary.

"Crocuses an' snowdrops an' daffydown-dillys. They'll poke up a bit higher here, and push out a spike more there, an' uncurl a leaf this day an' another that. You watch 'em."

"I am going to," said Mary.

Very soon she heard the soft rustling flight of the robin. He was very pert and lively.

"Do you think he remembers me?" she said.

"Remembers thee!" said Ben. "He knows every cabbage stump in th' gardens, let alone

th' people. Tha's no need to try to hide anything from *him*."

She walked away to outside the long, ivy-
covered wall over which she could see the
tree-tops; and the second time she walked up
and down the most interesting and exciting
thing happened to her, and it was all through
Ben Weatherstaff's robin.

She heard a chirp and a twitter, and when
she looked at the bare flower-bed at her left
side there he was hopping about. The flower-
bed was not quite bare, and as the robin
hopped about under the shrubs at the back of
the bed, she saw him hop over a small pile of
freshly turned up earth.

Mary looked at it, and saw something
almost buried in the newly turned soil. It was
something like a ring of rusty iron or brass,
and when the robin flew up into a tree nearby,
she put out her hand and picked the ring up. It
was more than a ring, however; it was an old
key which looked as if it had been buried a
long time.

"Perhaps it has been buried for ten years,"
she said in a whisper. "Perhaps it is the key to
the garden."

If it was the key to the closed garden, and
she could find out where the door was, she
could perhaps open it and see what was

inside the walls, and what had happened to the old rose-trees.

She put the key in her pocket and slowly walked up and down her walk looking at the wall, or, rather, at the ivy growing on it. Howsoever carefully she looked, she could see nothing but thickly growing, glossy, dark green leaves.

The next day when Martha returned from her visit home, Mary was surprised that Martha had brought her a present.

"A present!" exclaimed Mistress Mary. "How could a cottage full of fourteen hungry people give anyone a present!"

"A man was drivin' across the moor peddlin'," Martha explained. "An' Mother, she says to me: 'Martha, tha's brought thee thy wages like a good lass, an' I've got four places to put every penny, but I'm just going to take tuppence out of it to buy that child a skippin'-rope,' an' she bought one, an' here it is."

It was a strong, slender rope with a striped red and blue handle at each end, but Mary Lennox had never seen a skipping-rope before.

"What is it for?" she asked.

"For!" cried out Martha. "This is what it's for; just watch me."

And she ran into the middle of the room

and, taking a handle in each hand, began to skip, and skip, and skip, while Mary turned in her chair to stare at her.

"Your mother is a kind woman," said Mary. "Do you think I could ever skip like that?"

"You just try it," urged Martha. "You can't skip a hundred at first, but if you practice you'll mount up. Mother says: 'Let her play out in th' fresh air skippin' an' it'll stretch her legs an' arms an' give her some strength in 'em.'"

Mary opened the door to go out with the rope, and then suddenly thought of something and turned back.

"Martha," she said, "they were your wages. It was your twopence really. Thank you."

The skipping-rope was a wonderful thing. She counted and skipped, and skipped and counted, until her cheeks were quite red. Mary skipped round all the gardens and round the orchard, resting every few minutes. She stopped once and there, lo and behold, was the robin swaying on a long branch of ivy. He greeted her with a chirp.

"You showed me where the key was yesterday," she said to the robin. "You ought to show me the door today; but I don't believe you know!"

Mary Lennox had heard a great deal about

Magic in her Ayah's stories, and she always said what happened almost at that moment was Magic.

A nice little gust of wind rushed down the walk, and it was strong enough to sway the trailing sprays of untrimmed ivy hanging from the wall. Mary had stepped close to the robin, and suddenly the gust of wind swung aside some loose ivy trails, and more suddenly still she jumped towards it and caught it in her hand. She had seen something under it—a round knob which had been covered by the leaves hanging over it. It was the knob of a door.

She put her hands under the leaves and began to pull and push them aside. Thick as the ivy hung, it nearly all was a loose and swinging curtain, though some had crept over wood and iron. Mary's heart began to thump and her hands to shake a little in her delight and excitement.

She put her hand in her pocket, drew out the key, and found it fitted the keyhole. She put the key in and turned it. It took two hands to do it, but it did turn.

She held back the swinging curtain of ivy and pushed back the door which opened slowly—slowly.

Then she slipped through it, and shut it

behind her, and stood with her back against it, looking about her and breathing quite fast with excitement, and wonder, and delight.

She was standing *inside* the secret garden.

It was the sweetest, most mysterious-looking place anyone could imagine. The high walls which shut it in were covered with the leafless stems of climbing roses. All the ground was covered with grass of a wintry brown, and out of it grew clumps of bushes which were surely rose-bushes if they were alive. There were other trees in the garden, and one of the things which made the place look strangest and loveliest was that climbing roses had run all over them and swung down long tendrils which made light swaying curtains, and here and there they caught at each other or at a far-reaching branch and had crept from one tree to another and made lovely bridges of themselves. There were neither leaves nor roses on them now, and Mary did not know whether they were dead or alive. She walked under one of the fairy-like arches between the trees and looked up at the sprays and tendrils which formed them.

Everything was strange and silent, and she seemed to be hundreds of miles away from anyone, but somehow she did not feel lonely at all. All that troubled her was her wish that

She was standing *inside* the secret garden.

she knew whether all the roses were dead. If it were a quite alive garden, how wonderful it would be, and what thousands of roses would grow on every side.

She skipped round the whole garden, stopping when she wanted to look at things. At one alcove she stopped skipping. There had once been a flower-bed in it, and she thought she saw something sticking out of the black earth—some sharp little pale green points. She bent very close to them and sniffed the fresh scent of the damp earth. She liked it very much.

"Perhaps there are some other ones coming up in other places," she said. She went slowly and kept her eyes on the ground. She found ever so many more sharp, pale green points, and she became quite excited again. She did not know anything about gardening, but the grass seemed so thick in some of the places where the green points were pushing their way through that she thought they did not seem to have room enough to grow. She found a rather sharp piece of wood and knelt down and dug and weeded out the weeds and grass until she made nice little clear places around them.

She went from place to place, and dug and weeded, and enjoyed herself so immensely that she was led on from bed to bed and into the grass under the trees. Mistress Mary worked in her garden until it was time to go to her midday dinner. Then she ran lightly across the grass, pushed open the slow old door, and slipped through it under the ivy.

In the course of her digging with her pointed stick, Mistress Mary had found herself digging up a sort of white root rather like an onion. She now, back in her rooms, wondered if Martha could tell her what it was.

"Martha," she said, "what are those white roots that look like onions?"

"They're bulbs," answered Martha. "Lots o' spring flowers grow from 'em. Eh! they are nice. Dickon's got a whole lot of 'em planted in our bit o' garden."

"Does Dickon know all about them?" asked Mary.

"Our Dickon can make a flower grow out of a brick wall."

"Do bulbs live a long time? Would they live years and years if no one helped them?"

"They're things as helps themselves," said Martha. "If you don't trouble 'em, most of em'll work away underground for a lifetime an' spread out an' have little 'uns."

Mary had finished her dinner and gone to

her favorite seat on the hearth-rug. "I wish—I wish I had a little spade," she said. "If I had a little spade I could dig somewhere as Ben does, and I might make a little garden if he would give me some seeds. How much would a little spade cost—a little one?"

"Well," said Martha, "at Thwaite village there's a shop or so an' I saw little garden sets with a spade an' a rake an' a fork all tied together for two shillings."

"I've got more than that in my purse," said Mary. "Mrs. Medlock gives me one every Saturday. I didn't know what to spend it on."

"Now I've just thought of somethin'," said Martha. "In the shop at Thwaite they sell packages o' flower-seeds for a penny each, and our Dickon, he knows which is th' prettiest ones an' how to make 'em grow. We could write a letter to him an' ask him to go an' buy th' garden tools an' th' seeds at th' same time."

This was the letter Martha dictated to her:

My dear Dickon,
    This comes hoping to find you well as it leaves me at present. Miss Mary has plenty of money and will you go to Thwaite and buy her some flower seeds and a set of garden tools to make a flower-bed. Pick the prettiest ones and easy to grow because she has never

done it before and lived in India which is different. Give my love to Mother and every one of you.

Your loving sister,
Martha Phoebe Sowerby

The sun shone down for nearly a week on the secret garden. The Secret Garden was what Mary called it when she was thinking of it. She liked the name, and she liked still more the feeling that when its beautiful old walls shut her in, no one knew where she was.

She was an odd, determined little person, and, now that she had something interesting to be determined about, she was very much absorbed indeed. She worked and dug and pulled up weeds steadily. It seemed to her like a fascinating sort of play. She found many more of the sprouting pale green points than she had ever hoped to find. She wondered how long it would be before they showed that they were flowers.

During the week of sunshine, she became very intimate with Ben Weatherstaff. "Tha'rt like th' robin," he said to her one morning when he lifted his head and saw her standing by him. "I never knows when I shall see thee or which side tha'll come from."

Ben very seldom talked much and sometimes did not even answer Mary's questions
except by a grunt, but this morning he
said more than usual. "Tha's beginnin' to do
Misselthwaite credit," he said. "Tha's a bit
fatter than tha' was an' tha's not quite so
yeller. Tha's looked like a young plucked
crow when tha' first came into this garden a
month ago. Think I to myself I never set eyes
on an uglier, sourer-faced young 'un."

Mary was not vain, and as she had never
thought much of her looks, she was not
greatly disturbed.

"I know I'm fatter," she said. Then she
asked him, "When rose-trees have no leaves
and look gray and brown and dry, how can
you tell whether they are dead or alive?"

"Wait till th' spring gets at 'em—wait till th'
sun shines on th' rain an' th' rain falls on the
sunshine an' then tha'll find out.—Why does
tha' care so much about roses an' such, all of
a sudden?"

Mary was almost afraid to answer. "I—I
want to play that—that I have a garden of my
own," she stammered.

She stayed with him for ten or fifteen minutes longer and asked him as many questions
as she dared. When she persisted, however, in

her questions about the rose-trees, he got impatient with her and left.

So she went skipping slowly down the outside walk, thinking that here in Ben was another person whom she liked, in spite of his crossness.

There was a walk which curved round the secret garden and ended at a gate which opened into a wood in the park. She thought she would skip round this walk and look into the wood and see if there were any rabbits hopping about. When she reached the little gate she opened it and went through because she heard a low, peculiar whistling sound and wanted to find out what it was.

A boy was sitting under a tree, with his back against it, playing on a rough wooden pipe. He was a funny-looking boy about twelve. He looked very clean and his nose turned up and his cheeks were as red as poppies, and never had Mistress Mary seen such round and such blue eyes in any boy's face. And on the trunk of the tree he leaned against, a brown squirrel was clinging and watching him, and from behind a bush nearby a cock pheasant was delicately stretching his neck to peep out, and quite near him were two rabbits sitting up and sniffing—and it appeared as if they were all drawing near to watch him and listen to the strange, low, little call his pipe seemed to make.

When he saw Mary he held up his hand and spoke to her in a voice almost as low and rather like his piping. "Don't tha' move," he said. "It'd flight 'em."

He stopped playing his pipe and began to rise from the ground. He moved so slowly that it scarcely seemed as though he were moving.

"I'm Dickon," the boy said. "I know tha'rt Miss Mary."

Mary knew nothing about boys, and she felt rather shy.

"Did you get Martha's letter?" she asked.

"That's why I come.—I've got th' garden tools. There's a little spade an' rake an' a fork an' hoe. There's a trowel, too. An' th' woman in th' shop threw in a packet o' white poppy an' one o' blue larkspur when I bought th' other seeds."

"Will you show the seeds to me?" Mary said.

They sat down and he took a little brown-paper package out of his coat pocket. He untied the string and inside there were ever so many neater and small packages, with a picture of a flower on each one. He told her how to plant them, and watch them, and feed and water them. "See here," he said. "I'll plant them for thee myself. Where is tha' garden?"

Mary did not know what to say, so for a whole minute she said nothing.

"Tha's got a bit o' garden, hasn't tha'?" Dickon said.

"Could you keep a secret, if I told you one?"

"I'm keepin' secrets all th' time," he said. "If I couldn't keep secrets from th' other lads, secrets about foxes' cubs, an' birds' nests, an' wild things' holes, there'd be naught safe on th' moor. Aye, I can keep secrets."

"I've stolen a garden," she said very fast. "It isn't mine. It isn't anybody's. Nobody wants it, nobody cares for it, nobody ever goes into it. They're letting it die, all shut in by itself!" She threw her arms over her face and burst out crying—poor little Mistress Mary.

"Eh-h-h!" said Dickon.

"I've nothing to do," said Mary. "Nothing belongs to me. I found it and I got into it myself. I was only just like the robin, and they wouldn't take it from the robin."

"Where is it?"

"Come with me and I'll show you," she said.

When she brought him to the Secret Garden, Dickon looked round and round about it, and round and round again. "Eh! The nests as'll be here come springtime."

"Will there also be roses? I thought perhaps they were all dead."

"Eh! No! Not them—not all of 'em!—Look here."

He stepped over to the nearest tree. "There's lots o' dead wood as ought to be cut out," he said. "An' there's a lot o' old wood, but it made some new last year."

Dickon was working all the time he was telling Mary about gardening and she was following him and helping him with her fork or the trowel.

"There's a lot of work to do here!" he said.

"Will you come again and help me do it?" Mary begged. "I'm sure I can help, too. I can dig and pull up weeds, and do whatever you tell me. Oh! do come, Dickon!"

"I'll come every day if tha' wants me, rain or shine. It's th' best fun I ever had in my life— shut in here an' wakenin' up a garden."

"Dickon," Mary said. "You are as nice as Martha said you were."

When the big clock in the courtyard struck the hour of her midday dinner, Mary could scarcely bear to leave him.

"Whatever happens, you—you never would tell?" she said.

"If tha' was a missel thrush an' showed me where thy nest was, does tha' think I'd tell anyone? Not me," he said. "Tha' art as safe as a missel thrush."

And she was quite sure she was.

Mary ate her dinner as quickly as she could, and when she rose from the table she was going to run to her room to put on her hat again, but Martha stopped her.

"Mr. Craven came back this mornin' and I think he wants to see you," said Martha. "He's goin' away tomorrow for a long time. He mayn't come back till autumn or winter."

Mrs. Medlock walked in now. "Your hair's rough," she said to Mary. "Go and brush it. Martha, help her to slip on her best dress. Mr. Craven sent me to bring her to him in his study."

After her dress was changed, she was taken to a part of the house she had not been into before. Mrs. Medlock knocked at a door, and they entered the room together. A man was sitting in an arm-chair before the fire.

"This is Miss Mary, sir," said Mrs. Medlock. And then the housekeeper left the room.

Mary could see that the man in the chair was not so much a hunchback as a man with high, rather crooked shoulders, and he had black hair streaked with white.

"Come here," he said. "Are you well?"

"Yes," answered Mary.

"Do they take good care of you?"

"Yes."

"I forgot you," he said. "I intended to send you a governess or nurse or someone of that sort, but I forgot."

"I am—I am too big for a nurse," said Mary. "And please—please don't make me have a governess yet."

"Is there anything you want?"

"Might I have a bit of earth?"

"Earth!" he repeated. "What do you mean?"

"To plant seeds in—to make things grow—to see them come alive."

"Do you care about gardens so much? You remind me of someone else who loved the earth and things that grow. When you see a bit of earth you want, take it, child, and make it come alive."

He called Mrs. Medlock in and told her, "Mary must be less delicate before she begins lessons. Give her simple, healthy food. Let her run wild in the garden."

You never know what the weather will do in Yorkshire, particularly in the springtime. She was awakened in the night by the sound of rain beating with heavy drops against her window. The wind was "wuthering" round the corners and in the chimneys of the huge old house. Mary sat up in bed and felt miserable and angry.

How the wind "wuthered" and how the big raindrops poured down and beat against the pane! She had been lying awake for about an hour, when suddenly something made her sit up in bed and turn her head towards the door listening. She listened and listened. "It isn't the wind now," she said. "That isn't the wind. It is different. It is that crying that I heard before." She put her foot out of bed and stood on the floor.

"I am going to find out what it is," she said. There was a candle by her bedside and she took it up and went softly out of the room. The sound had come up that passage. The far-off, faint crying went on and led her.

She pushed the door open very gently and closed it behind her, and she stood in the corridor and could hear the crying quite plainly. She could see a glimmer of light coming from beneath a door, and so she walked to the door and pushed it open, and there she was standing in the room!

There was a low fire glowing on the hearth and a night-light burning by the side of a bed, and on the bed was lying a boy, crying piti-

On the bed was lying a boy, crying pitifully.

fully. The boy had a sharp, delicate face. Mary crept across the room, and as she drew nearer the light from her candle attracted the boy's attention and he turned his head on his pillow and stared at her.

"Who are you?" he said. "Are you a ghost?"

"No, I am not," Mary answered. "Are you one?"

"No," he replied. "I am Colin."

"Who is Colin?"

"I am Colin Craven. Who are you?"

"I am Mary Lennox. Mr. Craven is my uncle."

"He is my father," said the boy.

"Your father! No one ever told me he had a boy!"

"Come here," he said.

She came close to the bed and he put out his hand and touched her.

"You are real, aren't you?" he said.

"I will pinch you a little if you like, to show you how real I am. For a minute I thought you might be a dream, too."

"Where did you come from?" he asked.

"From my own room. The wind wuthered so I couldn't go to sleep and I heard someone crying and wanted to find out who it was. What were you crying for?"

"Because I couldn't go to sleep either, and my head ached."

"Did no one tell you I had come to live here?" asked Mary.

"No, they daren't. I should have been afraid you would see me. I am like this always, ill and having to lie down. The servants are not allowed to speak about me. If I live I may be a hunchback, but I shan't live. My father hates to think I may be like him."

"Oh, what a queer house this is!" Mary said. "Everything is a kind of secret. Rooms are locked up and gardens are locked up—and you! Have you been locked up?"

"No. I stay in this room because I don't want to be moved out of it. It tires me too much."

"Does your father come and see you?" Mary asked.

"Sometimes. Generally when I am asleep. My mother died when I was born and it makes him wretched to look at me."

"Have you been here always?"

"Nearly always. Sometimes I have been taken to places at the seaside, but I won't stay because people stare at me. I used to wear an iron thing to keep my back straight, but a grand doctor came from London to see me and said it was stupid. He told them to take it off and keep me out in the fresh air. I hate fresh air and I don't want to go out."

"I didn't when first I came here," said Mary.

"Sit down on that big footstool and talk. I want to hear about you."

"What do you want me to tell you?"

He wanted to know how long she had been at Misselthwaite; which corridor her room was on; what she had been doing; if she disliked the moor as he disliked it; where she had lived before she came to Yorkshire. She answered all these questions and many more, and he lay back on his pillow and listened.

"How old are you?" he asked.

"I am ten," answered Mary. "And so are you."

"How do you know that?"

"Because when you were born the garden door was locked and the key was buried. And it has been locked for ten years."

"What garden door was locked? Who did it? Where was the key buried?"

"It—it was the garden Mr. Craven hates. He locked the door. No one—no one knew where he buried the key."

He, like Mary, had had nothing to think about, and the idea of a hidden garden attracted him as it had attracted her. He asked question after question. Where was it? Had she never looked for the door? Had she never asked the gardeners?

"They won't talk about it," said Mary. "I think they have been told not to answer questions."

"I would make them," said Colin. "If I were to live, this place would sometime belong to me. They all know that. I would make them tell me."

"Oh, don't—don't—don't—don't do that!" she cried out.

"Why?"

"If you make them open the door and take you in like that it will never be a secret again. If no one knows but ourselves—if there was a door, hidden somewhere under the ivy—if there was—and we could find it; and if we could slip through it together and shut it behind us, and no one knew anyone was inside and we called it our garden, and if we played there almost every day and dug and planted seeds and made it all come alive. Oh, don't you see how much nicer it would be if it was a secret?"

"I should like that. I should not mind fresh air in a secret garden. What a lot of things you know. I feel as if you had been inside the garden."

She did not know what to say, so she did not say anything.

"I am going to let you look at something," he said. "Do you see that rose-colored silk curtain hanging on the wall over the mantelpiece? There is a cord hanging from it. Go and pull it."

The silk curtain uncovered a picture of a girl with a laughing face.

"She is my mother," said Colin. "If she had lived I believe I should not have been ill always. And my father would not have hated to look at me. I dare say I should have had a strong back. Draw the curtain again."

"Why is the curtain drawn over her?"

"I made them do it," he said. "Sometimes I don't like to see her looking at me. Besides, she is mine, and I don't want everyone to see her."

"Shall I go away now? Your eyes look sleepy."

"I wish I could go to sleep before you leave me. I am glad you came."

"Shut your eyes, and I will do what my Ayah used to do in India. I will pat your hand and stroke it and sing something quite low."

"That is nice," he said, and she went on chanting in Hindustani and stroking until he was fast asleep. She got up softly, took her candle, and crept away without making a sound.

The moor was hidden in mist when the morning came, and the rain had not stopped pouring down.

In the afternoon, Mary told Martha, "I have found out what the crying was."

"Tha' hasn't! Never!"

"I heard it in the night. And I got up and went to see where it came from. It was Colin. I found him. We talked and talked and he said he was glad I came."

"Art tha' sure? Tha' doesn't know what he's like when anything vexes him."

"He wasn't vexed," said Mary. "He wouldn't let me go. Before I left him I sang him to sleep."

"I can scarcely believe thee! If he'd been like he is most times he'd have throwed himself into one of his tantrums and roused th' house. He won't let strangers look at him. If Mrs. Medlock finds out, she'll think I broke orders and told thee and I shall be packed back to Mother."

"He is not going to tell Mrs. Medlock anything about it yet. It's to be a sort of secret just at first. And he wants me to come and talk to him every day. And you are to tell me when he wants me."

"Me!" said Martha. "I shall lose my place!"

"You can't if you are doing what he wants you to do and everybody is obliged to obey him."

"Does tha' mean to say, that he was nice to thee?"

"I think he almost liked me," Mary answered. "What is the matter with him?"

"Nobody knows for sure and certain," said Martha. "Mr. Craven went off his head like when he was born. It was because Mrs. Craven died. He wouldn't set eyes on th' baby. He just raved and said it'd be another hunchback like him and it'd better die."

"Is Colin a hunchback? He didn't look like one."

"He isn't yet," said Martha.

"Do you think he will die?"

"Mother says there's no reason why any child should live that gets no fresh air an' doesn't do nothin' but lie on his back an' read picture-books an' take medicine."

Martha heard the bell ring and she went to see Colin's nurse. She returned in about ten minutes. "Well, tha' has bewitched him," she said. "He's told the nurse to stay away until six o'clock. Th' minute she was gone he called me to him an' says: 'I want Mary Lennox to come and talk to me, and remember you're not to tell anyone.'"

There was a bright fire on the hearth when Mary entered Colin's room.

"Come in," he said. "I've been thinking about you all morning."

"I've been thinking about you, too," answered Mary. "I was thinking how different you are from Dickon."

"Who is Dickon? What a queer name!"

"He is Martha's brother. He is twelve years old. He is not like anyone else in the world. He can charm foxes and squirrels and birds. He plays a very soft tune on a pipe and they come and listen."

"Tell me some more about him. Does he like the moor?"

"When Dickon talks about it you feel as if you saw things and heard them, and as if you were standing in the heather with the sun shining and the gorse smelling like honey—and all full of bees and butterflies."

"You never see anything like that if you are ill," said Colin.

"You can't if you stay in your room," said Mary.

"How could I go on the moor? I am going to die."

"See here," said Mary. "Don't let us talk about dying; I don't like it. Let us talk about living. Let us talk and talk about Dickon."

It was the best thing she could have said. To talk about Dickon meant to talk about the moor and about Martha's family's cottage, and about Dickon's mother, and the skipping-rope, and the moor with the sun on it, and about pale green points sticking up out of the green sod. And it was all so alive Mary talked more than she had ever talked before—and Colin both talked and listened as he had never done either before. And they both began to laugh over nothing as children will when they are happy together.

"Do you know there is one thing we have never once thought of?" he said. "We are cousins."

It seemed so queer that they had talked so much and never remembered this simple thing that they laughed more than ever, because they had got into the humor to laugh at anything. And in the midst of the fun the door opened and in walked Dr. Craven, who was himself Mr. Craven's cousin, and Mrs. Medlock.

"Good Lord!" exclaimed Mrs. Medlock.

"What is this?" said Dr. Craven. "What does it mean?"

"This is my cousin, Mary Lennox," Colin said. "I asked her to come and talk to me. I like her. She must come and talk to me whenever I send for her.—She heard me crying and found me herself. I am glad she came."

Dr. Craven sat down by Colin and felt his pulse. "I am afraid there has been too much excitement. Excitement is not good for you, my boy."

"I should be excited if she kept away," answered Colin. "I am better. She makes me better. The nurse must bring up her tea with mine. We will have tea together."

After another week of rain, the high arch of blue sky appeared again and the sun which poured down was quite hot. Though there had been no chance to see either the secret garden or Dickon, Mistress Mary had enjoyed herself very much. She had spent hours of every day with Colin in his room, talking. They had looked at splendid books and pictures, and sometimes Mary had read things to Colin, and sometimes he had read a little to her.

In her talks with Colin, Mary had tried to be very cautious about the secret garden. As she began to like to be with him, she wanted to discover whether he was the kind of boy you could tell a secret to.

On that first morning when the sky was blue again, Mary wakened very early. "The little clouds are all pink," said Mary, "and I've never seen the sky look like this. I can't wait! I am going to see the garden!"

When she had reached the place where the door of the secret garden hid itself under the ivy, she was startled by the caw-caw of a crow, and when she looked up, there sat a big, glossy-plumaged, blue-black bird. When she got fairly into the garden, he had alighted on a dwarf apple-tree, and under the apple-tree was lying a little reddish animal with a bushy tail, and both of them were watching the stooping body and rust-red head of Dickon, who was kneeling on the grass working hard.

"Oh, Dickon! Dickon!" Mary cried out. "How could you get here so early! The sun has only just got up!"

He got up himself, laughing. "Eh!" he said. "I was up long before him. Th' world's all fair begun again this mornin'. When th' sun did jump up, th' moor went mad for joy, an' I run like mad myself. An' I come straight here."

Seeing him talking to a stranger, the little bushy-tailed animal rose from its place under the tree and came to him, and the rook, cawing once, flew down from its branch and settled quietly on his shoulder.

"This is th' little fox cub," he said, rubbing the little reddish animal's head. "It's named Captain. An' this bird here's Soot. Soot, he flew across th' moor with me, an' Captain he run same as if th' hounds had been after him. They both felt the same as I did."

Dickon and Mary ran from one part of the garden to another and found many wonders. He showed her swelling leaf-buds on rose branches which had seemed dead. He showed her ten thousand new green points pushing through the mold.

There was every joy on earth in the secret garden that morning.

While quietly watching the robin build his nest, Mary asked Dickon if he knew about Colin.

He asked in return, "What does tha' know about him?"

"I've seen him. I have been to talk to him every day this week. He says I'm making him forget about being ill and dying."

"I am glad o' that," Dickon exclaimed. "Everybody as knowed about Mester Craven knowed there was a little lad as was like to be a cripple, an' they knowed Mester Craven didn't like him to be talked about. He'd buy anythin' as money could buy for th' poor lad, but he'd like to forget he's on earth. For one

There was every joy on earth in the secret garden
that morning.

thing, he's afraid he'll look at Colin some day and find he's growed hunchback."

"Colin's so afraid of it himself that he won't sit up," said Mary. "He says he's always thinking that if he should feel a lump coming he should go crazy and scream himself to death."

"Eh! he oughtn't to lie there thinkin' things like that," said Dickon. "No lad could get well as thought them sort o' things.—If he was out here he wouldn't be watchin' for lumps to grow on his back; he'd be watchin' for buds to break on th' rose-bushes, an' he'd likely be healthier. I was wonderin' if us could ever get him in th' humor to come out here an' lie under th' trees in his carriage."

"He's been lying in his room so long and he's always been so afraid of his back that it has made him queer," said Mary. "He knows a good many things out of books, but he doesn't know anything else. But he likes to hear about this garden because it's a secret. I daren't tell him much, but he said he wanted to see it."

They found a great deal to do that morning, and Mary was late in returning to the house and was also in such a hurry to get back to her work that she quite forgot Colin until the last moment.

"Tell Colin that I can't come and see him yet," she said to Martha.

The afternoon was even lovelier and busier than the morning had been. When Dickon and Mary parted, the sun was beginning to set and sending deep gold-colored rays slanting under the trees.

"It'll be fine tomorrow," said Dickon. "I'll be at work by sunrise."

"So will I," said Mary.

She ran back to the house as quickly as her feet would carry her. She wanted to tell Colin about Dickon's fox cub and the rook and about what the springtime had been doing. But Martha was waiting for Mary with a doleful face.

"What is the matter?" Mary asked. "What did Colin say when you told him I couldn't come?"

"Eh!" said Martha. "I wish tha'd gone. He was nigh goin' into one o' his tantrums. There's been a nice to do all afternoon to keep him quiet."

He was not on his sofa when Mary went into his room. He was lying flat on his back in bed, and he did not turn his head towards her as she came in.

"Why didn't you get up?" she said.

"I did get up this morning when I thought you were coming," he answered, without looking at her. "I made them put me back in bed this afternoon. Why didn't you come?"

"I was working in the garden with Dickon," said Mary.

"I won't let that boy come here if you go and stay with him instead of coming to talk to me," he said.

"If you send Dickon away, I'll never come into this room again," she retorted.

"You'll have to if I want you," said Colin.

"I won't!" said Mary.

"I'll make you," said Colin. "They shall drag you in."

"Shall they!" said Mary. "They may drag me in, but they can't make me talk when they get me here. I'll sit and clench my teeth and never tell you one thing. I won't even look at you. I'll stare at the floor!"

"You are a selfish thing!" cried Colin.

"What are you?" said Mary. "Selfish people always say that. Anyone is selfish who doesn't do what they want. You're more selfish than I am. You're the most selfish boy I ever saw."

"I'm not," snapped Colin. "I'm not as selfish as your fine Dickon is! He keeps you playing in the dirt when he knows I am all by myself. He's selfish, if you like!"

"He's nicer than any other boy that ever lived!" she said. "He's—he's like an angel!"

"A nice angel!" Colin sneered. "He's a common cottage boy off the moor!"

"He's better than a common rajah!" retorted Mary. A rajah is an Indian prince, which is what Mary sometimes thought of Colin as being like. "He's a thousand times better!"

"I'm not as selfish as you, because I'm always ill, and I'm sure there is a lump coming on my back," he said. "And I am going to die besides."

"You're not!" contradicted Mary.

"I'm not?" he cried. "I am! You know I am! Everybody says so."

"I don't believe it," said Mary. "You just say that to make people sorry. If you were a nice boy it might be true—but you're too nasty!"

Colin sat up. "Get out of this room!" he shouted.

"I'm going," Mary said. "And I won't come back!—I was going to tell you all sorts of nice things. Dickon brought his fox and his rook and I was going to tell you all about them. Now I won't tell you a single thing!"

Mary went back to her room not feeling at all as she had felt when she had come in from the garden. She was cross and disappointed, but not at all sorry for Colin.

She had got up very early in the morning and had worked hard in the garden, and she was tired and sleepy, so as soon as Martha had brought her supper and she had eaten it, she was glad to go to bed.

She thought it was the middle of the night when she was awakened by such dreadful sounds that she jumped out of bed in an instant. "It's Colin," she said. "He's having one of those tantrums. How awful it sounds." She put her hands over her ears and felt sick and shivering.

Just then she heard feet running down the corridor, and her door opened and the nurse came in.

"He's working himself into hysterics," she said in a hurry. "He'll do himself harm. No one can do anything with him. You come and try. He likes you."

"He turned me out of the room this evening," said Mary.

"You go and scold him. Give him something new to think of."

Mary flew along the corridor, and the nearer she got to the screams the higher her own temper mounted. She felt quite wicked by the time she reached the door. She slapped it open with her hand and ran across the room to the bed.

"You stop!" she almost shouted. "You stop! I hate you! Everybody hates you! I wish every-body would run out of the house and let you scream yourself to death! You *will* scream yourself to death in a minute, and I wish you would!"

He had been lying on his face beating his pillow with his hands, and he actually almost jumped around, he turned so quickly at the sound of the furious little voice. His face looked dreadful, white and red, and swollen, and he was gasping and choking; but savage little Mary did not care an atom.

"If you scream another scream," she said, "I'll scream, too—and I can scream louder than you can, and I'll frighten you, I'll frighten you!"

"I can't stop!" he gasped, and sobbed. "I can't—I can't!"

"You can!" shouted Mary. "Half that ails you is hysterics and temper!"

"I felt the lump—I felt it," choked out Colin. "I shall have a hunch in my back and then I shall die," and he began to writhe and turned on his face and sobbed and wailed, but he didn't scream.

"You didn't feel a lump," said Mary. "If you did it was only a hysterical lump. There's nothing the matter with your horrid back— nothing but hysterics! Turn over and let me look at it."

It was a poor, thin back to look at when it

was bared. Mary looked up and down his spine, and down and up, as intently as if she had been the great doctor from London.

"There's not a single lump there!" she said at last. "There's not a lump as big as a pin—except backbone lumps, and you can only feel them because you're so thin. There's not a lump as big as a pin. If you ever say there is again, I shall laugh!"

"I didn't know," said the nurse coming forward, "that he thought he had a lump on his spine. I could have told him there was no lump there."

"C-could you?" he said pathetically.

"Yes, sir."

"Do you think—I could—live to grow up?" he said.

The nurse answered, "You probably will if you will do what you are told to do, and not give way to your temper, and stay out a great deal in the fresh air."

Colin's tantrum had passed and he was weak and worn out with crying, and this perhaps made him feel gentle. He put out his hand towards Mary, and, her own tantrum having passed, she was softened too, and met him half-way with her hand, so that it was a sort of making up.

"I'll—I'll go out with you, Mary," he said. "I

shall like to go out with you if Dickon will come and push my chair. I do so want to see Dickon and the fox and the crow."

"Would you like me to sing you that song I learned from my Ayah?" Mary whispered to Colin.

"Oh, yes!" he answered.

"I will put him to sleep," Mary said to the nurse. "You can go if you like."

The nurse was out of the room in a minute.

Colin asked, "Have you found out anything at all about the way into the secret garden?"

"Ye-es," she answered. "I think I have. And if you will go to sleep I will tell you tomorrow."

"Oh, Mary!" he said. "Oh, Mary! If I could go into it I think I should live to grow up!"

Of course, Mary did not waken early the next morning. She slept late because she was tired, and when Martha brought her breakfast she told her that though Colin was quite quiet, he was ill and feverish, as he always was after he had worn himself out with a fit of crying.

She had her hat on when she appeared in Colin's room. He was in bed, and his face was pitifully white and there were dark circles round his eyes.

"I'm glad you came," he said. "Are you going somewhere?"

"I won't be long," she said. "I'm going to

Dickon, but I'll come back. Colin, it's something about the secret garden."

His whole face brightened. "Oh! is it? I dreamed about it all night. I'll lie and think about it until you come back."

In five minutes Mary was with Dickon in their garden. The fox and the crow were with him again, and this time he had brought two tame squirrels.

"I came over on the pony this mornin'," he said. "Eh! he is a good little chap—Jump is! I brought these two in my pockets. This here one he's called Nut an' this here other one's called Shell."

When they sat down on the grass with Captain curled at their feet, Soot listening on a tree and Nut and Shell nosing about close to them, it seemed to Mary that it would be scarcely bearable to leave such delightfulness, but when she began to tell her story she could see he felt sorrier for Colin than she did.

"Eh! my! we mun get him out here—we mun get him watchin' an' listenin' and sniffin' up th' air an' get him just soaked through wi' sunshine."

Mary loved his broad Yorkshire dialect, and had, in fact, been trying to learn to speak it herself.

"Aye, that we mun," she said (which meant "Yes, indeed, we must"). "He wants to see thee and he wants to see Soot an' Captain. When I go back to the house to talk to him I'll ax him if tha' canna come an' see him tomorrow mornin'—an' bring the creatures wi' thee—and then—in a bit, when there's more leaves out, we'll get him to come out an' tha' shall push him in his chair an' we'll bring him here an' show him everything."

The garden had reached the time when every day and every night it seemed as if Magicians were passing through it drawing loveliness out of the earth and the boughs with wands. When she went back to the house and sat down close to Colin's bed he began to sniff.

"You smell like flowers and—and fresh things," he cried out.

"It's th' wind from th' moor," said Mary. "It comes o' sittin' on th' grass under a tree wi' Dickon an' wi' Captain an' Soot an' Nut an' Shell. It's th' springtime an' out o' doors an' sunshine as smells so graidely."

She said it as broadly as she could, and Colin began to laugh.

"What are you doing?" he said. "How funny it sounds."

"I'm givin' thee a bit o' Yorkshire," answered

Mary. "Doesn't tha' understand a bit o' York-shire when tha' hears it? An' tha' a Yorkshire lad thysel' bred an' born! Eh! I wonder tha'rt not ashamed o' thy face."

And then she began to laugh too, and they both laughed. There was so much to talk about. It seemed as if Colin could never hear enough of Dickon and his animals.

"I shouldn't mind Dickon looking at me," said Colin. "I want to see him."

"I'm glad you said that," said Mary. "Can I trust you? I trusted Dickon because birds trusted him. Can I trust you—for sure—*for sure?*"

"Yes—yes!"

"Well, Dickon will come to see you tomor-row morning and he'll bring his creatures with him."

"Oh! Oh!" Colin cried out in delight.

"But that's not all. The rest is better. There is a door into the garden. It is under the ivy on the wall."

"Oh! Mary!" he cried out. "Shall I see it? Shall I *live* to get into it?"

"Of course you'll see it!" snapped Mary. "Of course you'll live to get into it. Don't be silly!"

The next day Dickon visited Colin as prom-ised. The new-born lamb was in his arms and the little red fox trotted by his side. Nut sat on his left shoulder and Soot on his right, and Shell's head and paws peeped out of his coat pocket.

Dickon walked over to Colin's sofa and put the new-born lamb quietly on his lap, and immediately the little creature turned to the warm velvet dressing-gown and began to nuzzle and nuzzle into its folds and butt its tight-curled head with soft impatience against his side.

"What is it doing?" cried Colin. "What does it want?"

"It wants its mother," said Dickon. "I brought it to thee a bit hungry because I knowed tha'd like to see it feed."

Dickon knelt down by the sofa and took a feeding bottle from his pocket. Later, they looked at pictures in the gardening books and Dickon knew all the flowers by their country names and knew exactly which ones were already growing in the secret garden.

"I'm going to see them," cried Colin. "I am going to see them!"

"Aye, that tha' mun," said Mary. "An' tha' munnot lose no time about it."

But they were obliged to wait more than a week because first there came some very windy days and then Colin was threatened with a cold. Almost every day Dickon came in, if only for a few minutes, to talk about what was happening on the moor.

The most absorbing thing to think about, however, was the preparations to be made before Colin could be transported with sufficient secrecy to the garden. And then the day finally came where he was ready to go out. He had ordered the gardeners to stay away from the Long Walk by the garden walls that afternoon until Colin sent his word that they might go back to their work.

The strongest footman in the house carried Colin downstairs and put him in his wheeled-chair, near which Dickon waited outside. Dickon began to push the wheeled-chair. Mistress Mary walked beside it and Colin leaned back and lifted his face to the sky.

When they got into the secret garden, Colin looked round and round and round as Dickon and Mary had done. Over walls and earth and trees and swinging sprays and tendrils the fair green veil of tender little leaves had crept, and in the grass under the trees and the gray urns in the alcoves and here and there everywhere, were touches or splashes of gold and purple and white, and there were fluttering of wings and faint sweet pipes and humming and scents and scents. And the sun fell warm upon his face like a hand with a lovely touch.

And in wonder Mary and Dickon stood and stared at him. He looked so strange and different because a pink glow of color had actually crept all over him.

That morning, Mary and Dickon worked a little here and there and Colin watched them. They brought him things to look at—buds which were opening, buds which were tight closed, bits of twig whose leaves were just showing green, the feather of a woodpecker which had dropped on the grass, the empty shell of some bird early hatched. Every moment of the afternoon was full of new things and every hour the sunshine grew more golden.

"I don't want this afternoon to go," said Colin; "but I shall come back tomorrow, and the day after, and the day after, and the day after. I've seen the spring now and I'm going to see the summer. I'm going to see everything grow here. I'm going to grow here myself."

"That tha' will," said Dickon. "Us'll have thee walkin' about here an' diggin' same as other folk afore long."

"Walk!" said Colin. "Dig! Shall I?"

"For sure tha' will. Tha's got legs o' thine own, same as other folks!"

"Nothing really ails them," said Colin, "but they are so thin and weak. They shake so that

I'm afraid to try to stand on them."

"When tha' stops bein' afraid tha'lt stand on 'em," Dickon said.

"I shall?" said Colin, and he lay still, as if he were wondering about things.

In the midst of this stillness it was rather startling when Colin half lifted his head and exclaimed: "Who is that man?"

Mary and Dickon wheeled about and looked. There was Ben Weatherstaff's face glaring at them over the wall from the top of a ladder! Colin commanded Dickon to wheel him over to the wall under Ben Weatherstaff. Ben saw the boy in the wheeled-chair and his jaw dropped.

"Do you know who I am?" demanded Colin.

"Who tha' art?" he said. "Aye, that I do—wi' tha' mother's eyes starin' at me out o' tha' face. Tha'rt th' poor cripple."

"I'm not a cripple!" Colin cried out.

"Tha'—tha' hasn't got a crooked back?" Ben said.

"No!"

"Tha'—tha' hasn't got crooked legs?"

Colin began to tear the coverings off his lower limbs and disentangled himself. There was a brief, fierce scramble, the rugs were tossed on to the ground, Dickon held Colin's arm, the thin legs were out, the thin feet were

"I'm not a cripple!" Colin cried out.

on the grass. Colin was standing upright—his head thrown back and his strange eyes flashing lightning.

"Look at me!" he said at Ben.

Tears ran down Ben's weather-wrinkled cheeks. "Eh! Tha'rt as thin as a lath an' as white as a wraith, but there's not a knob on thee. Tha'lt make a mon yet. God bless thee!"

"I'm your master, Weatherstaff, when my father is away," said rajah Colin. "And you are to obey me. This is my garden. Don't dare to say a word about it! You get down from that ladder and go out to the Long Walk and Miss Mary will meet you and bring you here. You will have to be in the secret."

When his head was out of sight, Mary ran across the grass to the door under the ivy to meet Ben. And then when Ben came through the door in the wall he saw Colin standing by a tree.

"Am I a hunchback?" asked Colin. "Have I got crooked legs?"

"Not tha'," Ben said.

"What work do you do in the gardens, Weatherstaff?"

"Anythin' I'm told to do," answered old Ben. "I'm kep' on by favor—because tha' mother liked me."

"This was her garden, wasn't it?"

"Aye, it was that! She were main fond of it."

"It is my garden now. I am fond of it. I shall come here every day. But it is to be a secret. My orders are that no one is to know that we come here. Dickon and my cousin have worked and made it come alive. I shall send for you sometimes to help—but you must come when no one can see you."

"I've come here before when no one saw me," he said. "The last time I was here was about two year' ago."

"But no one has been in it for ten years!" cried Colin. "There was no door!"

"I come over th' wall," said old Ben. "Th' rheumatics held me back th' last two year'. She was so fond of it—she was! She says to me once, 'Ben, if ever I'm ill or if I go away you must take care of my roses.' When she did go away th' orders was no one was ever to come nigh. But I come."

Colin picked up Mary's trowel, and they watched him drive the end of it into the soil and turn some over. They all helped him plant a rose bush that afternoon.

Dr. Craven had been waiting some time at the house when they returned to it. "You should not have stayed so long," he said.

"I am not tired at all," said Colin. "It has made me well. Tomorrow I am going out in the morning as well as in the afternoon."

"I am not sure that I can allow it," answered Dr. Craven.

"It would not be wise to try to stop me," said Colin. "I am going."

Even Mary had found out that one of Colin's chief peculiarities was that he did not know in the least what a rude little brute he was with his way of ordering people about. "I am rather sorry for Dr. Craven," she told Colin. "It must have been very horrid to have had to be polite for ten years to a boy who was always rude. I would never have done it."

"Am I rude?" Colin inquired.

"Yes," answered Mary, "very. It is always having your own way that has made you so queer. But you needn't be cross. Because so am I queer—and so is Ben Weatherstaff. But I am not as queer as I was before I began to like people and before I found the garden."

"I don't want to be queer," said Colin. "I shall stop being queer if I go every day to the garden. There is Magic in there."

They always called it Magic, and indeed it seemed like it in the months that followed—the wonderful months—the radiant months—the amazing ones. Oh! the things that happened in that garden!

The seeds Dickon and Mary had planted grew as if fairies had tended them. And the roses—the roses! Rising out of the grass, tangled round the sun-dial, wreathing the tree-trunks, and hanging from their branches, climbing up the walls and spreading over them with long garlands falling in cascades—they came alive day by day, hour by hour. Fair, fresh leaves, and buds—and buds—tiny at first, but swelling and working Magic until they burst and uncurled into cups of scent delicately spilling themselves over their brims and filling the garden air.

Colin saw it all, watching each change as it took place. Every morning he was brought out and every hour of each day, when it didn't rain, he spent in the garden working, walking, and exercising.

"No one is to know anything about it until I have grown so strong that I can walk and run like any other boy. I shall come here every day in my chair and I shall be taken back in it. I won't have people whispering and asking questions and I won't let my father hear about it until the experiment has quite succeeded. Then some time when he comes back to Misselthwaite I shall just walk into his study and say: 'Here I am: I am like any other boy. I am quite well and I shall live to be a man.'"

The Secret Garden bloomed and bloomed and every morning revealed new miracles. In the robin's nest there were eggs and the robin's mate sat upon them, keeping them warm with her feathery breast and careful wings.

One morning while Colin, Mary, and Dickon were working in the garden, Colin stood up and stretched himself out to his tallest height and he threw out his arms exultantly.

"Mary! Dickon!" he cried. "Just look at me!"

They stopped their weeding and looked at him.

"Do you remember that first morning you brought me in here?"

"Aye, that we do," said Dickon.

"Just this minute," said Colin, "all at once I remembered it myself—when I looked at my hand digging with the trowel—and I had to stand up on my feet to see if it was real. And it *is* real! I'm *well*—I'm *well!*" He had known it before in a way, but just at that minute the realization had been so strong that he could not help calling out.

Later that morning Colin saw that the door in the ivied wall had been pushed gently open and a woman had entered. The ivy was behind her, the sunlight drifting through the trees and dappling her long blue cloak, and her nice fresh face smiling across the greenery. She had wonderful affectionate eyes. "Who is it?" wondered Colin.

Dickon cried out, "It's Mother!" And he went across the grass at a run. "I asked her to come!"

Colin began to move towards Mrs. Sowerby, too, and Mary went with him.

Colin held out his hand towards her. "Even when I was ill I wanted to see you, you and Dickon and the secret garden. I'd never wanted to see anyone or anything before. Are you surprised because I am so well?" Colin asked.

She put her hand on his shoulder and smiled. "Aye, that I am! but tha'rt so like thy mother tha' made my heart jump."

Next she turned to Mary and put both hands on Mistress Mary's shoulders and looked her little face over in a motherly fashion. "An' thee, too!" she said. "Tha'rt grown hearty. I'll warrant tha'rt like thy mother, too. Tha'lt be like a blush-rose when tha' grows up, my little lass, bless thee."

Susan Sowerby went round the garden with them and was told the whole story of it and shown every bush and tree which had come alive. Colin walked on one side of her and Mary on the other. Each of them kept looking up at her comfortable, rosy face, secretly curious about the delightful feeling she gave them.

She had packed a basket which held a regular feast this morning, and when the hungry hour came and Dickon brought it out from its hiding place, she sat down with them under their tree and watched them devour their food. She was full of fun and made them laugh at all sorts of things.

She got up at last to return to the house. It was time for Colin to be wheeled back also. But before he got into his chair, he told her, "You were just what I—what I wanted. I wish you were my mother—as well as Dickon's!"

All at once Susan Sowerby bent down and drew him with her warm arms close against the bosom under the blue cloak—as if he had been Dickon's brother.

"Eh! dear lad! Thy own mother's in this 'ere very garden, I do believe. She couldna' keep out of it. Thy father mun come back to thee— he mun!"

While the secret garden was coming alive and two children were coming alive with it, Colin's father, Archibald Craven, was wandering about certain far-away beautiful places in the Norwegian fjords, and the valleys and mountains of Switzerland. For ten years he had kept his mind filled with dark and heartbroken thinking.

But as golden summer changed into the

deeper golden autumn, he began to think of Misselthwaite and wonder if he should not go home. Now and then he wondered about his boy.

One night he had a dream. He thought that as he sat and breathed in the scent of the late roses and listened to the lapping of the water at his feet, he heard a voice calling. It was sweet and clear and happy and he heard it as distinctly as if it had been at his side.

"Archie! Archie! Archie!"

"Lilias! Lilias!" he answered. "Lilias! where are you?"

"In the garden," it came back like a sound from a golden flute. "In the garden!"

And then the dream ended. But he did not awaken. He slept soundly and sweetly all through the lovely night. When he did awake at last it was brilliant morning and a servant was standing staring at him. The man held a salver with some letters on it and he waited quietly until Mr. Craven took them.

He saw that the one laying at the top of the rest was an English letter and came from Yorkshire. He opened it.

Dear Sir,

I am Susan Sowerby, Martha and Dickon's mother, that lives nearby you in Yorkshire. I will make bold to tell you, sir, I would come

home if I was you. I think you would be glad
to come and—if you will excuse me, sir—I
think your lady would ask you to come if she
was here,

Your obedient servant,
Susan Sowerby

Mr. Craven read the letter twice before he
put it back in its envelope. He thought about
his dream.

"I will go back at once to Misselthwaite," he
said.

In a few days he was in Yorkshire again, and
on his railroad journey he found himself
thinking of his boy as he had never thought in
all the ten years past. He had not meant to be
a bad father, but he had not felt like a father
at all.

The drive across the wonderfulness of the
moor was a soothing thing. Why did it seem to
give him a sense of homecoming which he
had been sure he could never feel again? How
real that dream had been—how wonderful
and clear the voice which had called back to
him, "In the garden—In the garden!"

When he arrived at the Manor, he asked
Mrs. Medlock, "How is Master Colin?"

"Sir," she answered, "he's growing very
peculiar—when you compare him with what
he used to be. Just without warning—not long

after one of his worst tantrums, he suddenly insisted on being taken out every day by Miss Mary and Susan Sowerby's boy, Dickon, that could push his chair. He took a fancy to both Miss Mary and Dickon, and Dickon brought his tame animals, and, if you'll credit it, sir, out of doors he will stay from morning until night."

"Where is Master Colin now?" Mr. Craven asked.

"In the garden, sir. He's always in the garden—though not a human creature is allowed to go near for fear they'll look at him."

"In the garden!" Mr. Craven said, and after he had sent Mrs. Medlock away, he stood and repeated it again and again. "In the garden!"

He went out and crossed the lawn and turned into the Long Walk by the ivied walls. He felt as if he were being drawn back to the place he had so long forsaken. He knew where the door was, even though the ivy hung over it—and when he paused on the walk near the door, inside the garden there were sounds.

There was a quick, strong, young breathing and a wild outbreak of laughing shouts—and the door in the wall was flung wide open, the sheet of ivy swinging back, and a boy burst

A boy burst through the door at full speed.

through it at full speed and, without seeing the outsider, dashed almost into his arms.

Mr. Craven had extended his arms just in time to save the boy from falling. He was a tall boy and a handsome one. But it was the boy's eyes which made Mr. Craven gasp for breath.

Colin had never thought of such a meeting. And yet to come dashing out—winning a race—perhaps it was even better. Mary had been running with him and had dashed through the door too.

"Father," he said, "I'm Colin. You can't believe it. I scarcely can myself, I'm Colin."

"In the garden! In the garden!"

"Yes," said Colin. "It was the garden that did it—and Mary and Dickon and the creatures—and the Magic." Colin put out his hand and laid it on his father's arm. "Aren't you glad, Father?"

Mr. Craven put his hands on both the boy's shoulders and held him still. "Take me into the garden, my boy. And tell me all about it."

And so they led him in.

The place was a wilderness of autumn gold and purple and violet and flaming scarlet. Late roses climbed and hung and clustered, and the sunshine deepening the hue of the yellowing trees made one feel that one stood in a temple of gold.

"I thought it would be dead," said Mr. Craven.

"Mary thought so at first," said Colin. "But it came alive."

Then they sat down under their tree—all but Colin, who wanted to stand while he told the story.

"Now," he said at the end of the story, "it need not be a secret any more. I dare say it will frighten them nearly into fits when they see me—but I am never going to get into the chair again. I shall walk back with you, Father—to the house."

When Mrs. Medlock looked out from the kitchen towards the lawn she gave a little shriek, and every man and woman servant within hearing bolted across the servants' hall and stood looking through the window with their eyes almost staring out of their heads.

Across the lawn came the Master of Misselthwaite, and he looked as many of them had never seen him. And by his side, with his head up in the air, walked as strongly and steadily as any boy in Yorkshire—Master Colin!

CHILDREN'S THRIFT CLASSICS

Just $1.00
All books complete and unabridged, except where noted.
96pp., 5³⁄₁₆″ × 8¹⁄₄″, paperbound.

AESOP'S FABLES, Aesop. 28020-9

THE LITTLE MERMAID AND OTHER FAIRY TALES, Hans Christian Andersen. 27816-6

THE UGLY DUCKLING AND OTHER FAIRY TALES, Hans Christian Andersen. 27081-5

THE THREE BILLY GOATS GRUFF AND OTHER READ-ALOUD STORIES, Carolyn Sherwin Bailey (ed.). 28021-7

THE STORY OF PETER PAN, James M. Barrie and Daniel O'Connor. 27294-X

ROBIN HOOD, Bob Blaisdell. 27573-6

THE ADVENTURES OF BUSTER BEAR, Thornton W. Burgess. 27564-7

THE ADVENTURES OF CHATTERER THE RED SQUIRREL, Thornton W. Burgess. 27399-7

THE ADVENTURES OF DANNY MEADOW MOUSE, Thornton W. Burgess. 27565-5

THE ADVENTURES OF GRANDFATHER FROG, Thornton W. Burgess. 27400-4

THE ADVENTURES OF JERRY MUSKRAT, Thornton W. Burgess. 27817-4

THE ADVENTURES OF JIMMY SKUNK, Thornton W. Burgess. 28023-3

THE ADVENTURES OF PETER COTTONTAIL, Thornton W. Burgess. 26929-9

THE ADVENTURES OF POOR MRS. QUACK, Thornton W. Burgess. 27818-2

THE ADVENTURES OF REDDY FOX, Thornton W. Burgess. 26930-2

THE SECRET GARDEN, Frances Hodgson Burnett. (abridged) 28024-1

PICTURE FOLK-TALES, Valery Carrick. 27083-1

THE STORY OF POCAHONTAS, Brian Doherty (ed.). 28025-X

SLEEPING BEAUTY AND OTHER FAIRY TALES, Jacob and Wilhelm Grimm. 27084-X

THE ELEPHANT'S CHILD AND OTHER JUST SO STORIES, Rudyard Kipling. 27821-2

HOW THE LEOPARD GOT HIS SPOTS AND OTHER JUST SO STORIES, Rudyard Kipling. 27297-4

MOWGLI STORIES FROM "THE JUNGLE BOOK," Rudyard Kipling. 28030-6

NONSENSE POEMS, Edward Lear. 28031-4

BEAUTY AND THE BEAST AND OTHER FAIRY TALES, Marie Leprince de Beaumont and Charles Perrault. 28032-2

A DOG OF FLANDERS, Ouida (Marie Louise de la Ramée). 27087-4

PETER RABBIT AND 11 OTHER FAVORITE TALES, Beatrix Potter. 27845-X